THE APPLE
IN THE ORCHARD

1366B99ks 1

Canada

ONTARIO ARTS COUNCIL
CONSEIL DES ARTS DE L'ONTARIO

an Ontario government agency
un organisme du gouvernement de l'Ontario

Canada Council   Conseil des arts
for the Arts   du Canada

Guernica Editions Inc. acknowledges the support of
the Canada Council for the Arts and the Ontario Arts Council.
The Ontario Arts Council is an agency of the Government of Ontario.

We acknowledge the financial support of the Government of Canada.

THE APPLE
IN THE ORCHARD

BRIAN DEDORA

An imprint of Guernica Editions

TORONTO—CHICAGO—BUFFALO—LANCASTER (U.K.)

2024

Guernica founder: Antonio D'Alfonso
General editor: Michael Mirolla
1366 Books editor: Stuart Ross
Interior design & typesetting: Stuart Ross
Cover & 1366 logo design: Underline Studio
Author and pond-ring photos: Adrian Fortesque

Guernica Editions Inc.
1241 Marble Rock Rd., Gananoque, ON K7G 2V4
2250 Military Road, Tonawanda, NY 14150-6000 USA
www.guernicaeditions.com

Distributors:
Independent Publishers Group (IPG), 600 North Pulaski Rd., Chicago IL 60624
University of Toronto Press Distribution (UTP), 5201 Dufferin St., Toronto Ontario M3H 5T8

First edition. Printed in Canada.
Legal Deposit—First Quarter

Library of Congress Catalog Card Number: 2023947631
Library and Archives Canada Cataloguing in Publication
Title: The apple in the orchard / Brian Dedora.
Names: Dedora, B. (Brian), author.
Description: Series statement: 1366 books ; 1
Identifiers: Canadiana (print) 20230550274 | Canadiana (ebook) 20230550304 | ISBN 9781771838603 (softcover) | ISBN 9781771838610 (EPUB)
Subjects: LCGFT: Novels.
Classification: LCC PS8557.E28 A67 2024 | DDC C813/.54—dc23

Expert twist of the fine-wine bottle
to propel the drip around its rim,
to expend itself, as a wet
glaze upon its lip…

The little green apple

The city mad with money, you shake the tree, cash lands at your feet. You find a restaurant, you call it home, you "vant to be alone," you're owed a favour, you stop by. You're set up at the bar with a white linen napkin, cutlery. You listen, watch, are part of a night out, sit back on your stool, attend to the theatre: the grand welcoming by the maître d' ushering couples and groups to tables, special seats, choice spots, best views. Waiters ceremonially whisk off fur coats from gracious white-toothed smiles. Jewels from necks and wrists catch in the subdued light. Pulling back chairs for the just-right seating arrangements or along the banquettes, who would sit out or in, who could you see, best vantage point, settling tonight's guests. A drink before dinner, a recitation of this night's specials, he snaps deftly and with aplomb the *carte de menu* before the set plates. Murmurs of approval, the novelty of selections: arborio rice cakes, purple potatoes, *entrecôte* with a rosebud of butter, a pinch of *sel de mer*, desserts scribbled Jackson Pollock–like with chocolate syrup, dustings of powdered sugar, as the crystal-clear tinkling of wineglasses and silverware fills the room through a babble of voices becoming but one sound, one hive, one buzz.

You sit blessedly alone, separate, at the bar laid especially for you, as you are known, familiar, cross-talking with the barman, waiters as they come and go, fuelling the evening with a relaxation of measured ounces of cocktails, wine, champagne, reserved bottles from an extensive cellar, proffered and accepted, lifted by soft, sculptured, well-cared-for hands. Smiles, nods of appreciation of a nose, a palate, a finish with perfect combinations, apt pairings, subtle suggestions, continued pourings by the adept hands of chosen waiters ever wary of the emptying glass to be refilled, to move the evening along, to give it lift, to round it out, to get the cash...

To be in the press but not of it, listen to the chatter, endearments, encomiums. A flutter of hands: touches, pets, pats, slides over shoulders, a brush of cheek. A birthday boy finds buried in his salad of radicchio, endive, Boston bibb, cherry tomatoes run with rivulets of vinaigrette thickened with raw egg, a gold bracelet now twinkling from the end of his fork. A waiter passes with another fur coat folded ever so gently over his arm, to be hung with care in the hopes that St. Nicholas—

Goddammit, pay attention!

In the special cloakroom far away from the protesters in the street, who, with spray bombs and chants concerning the rights of animals to wear their skins, descend on the women, wives, mistresses stepping over curbs of snow in their taxi shoes from the back seats of black chrome and tinted-window automobiles, defended by hand-picked valets who push, shove, tear up placards and banners to roughly take back cans of spray paint, shooting lime green and fluorescents into the faces, snarls, howls of protesters while the maître d' beckons, welcomes, kisses, lends a helping hand to the perfectly coiffed now dusted with snow that catches the light, to glisten in the highlights of their hair.

Too soon this smoothed surface floating on the rising perceptible and the flood tide of alcohol will ripple ever so gently as the gremlin of a Chuck Berry duckwalk with his erectional guitar shakes, rattles, rolls to break the plain in crests, waves, and finally whitecaps of the storm that lies within, just beneath the surface of things. All jewels, pert designer dresses, suits, ties, shoes falling will arrive at the place of their intended and seductive destination beside a bed.

On your bars tool before the bar set with a white linen napkin and polished silver, flute bubbling light gold champagne above the fray, observant, solitary, a peacock fed on the hauteur of arrogance, a slight breeze blows through your hair, you extend as balm your hands, milk of kindness blesses the words issuing from your lips, engenders the contempt at your desk in the bookstore signing as if you know something, some gem, some key passage we want to know, the knowing of thyself juggling balls, pins, Frisbees divert the eye for the magician's sleight of hand, inestimable researcher, veritable sleuth.

The curtain is about to rise, sidewalks cleared of snow for the black-with-chrome-aplenty sedans with tinted windows, to open wide their back doors, to see alight slender and tenderly the stockinged ankle above the taxi shoe, the come-fuck-me pump, and the odd sensible leftist shoette (to keep up the demographic structures). Where the doorman greets, shakes, smiles, opens the front door while nimble, effusive, deft-fingered staff slip mink wolf Blackglama from shoulders to be stored securely in the specially adapted, air-controlled cloakroom, where the furs are hung with care in the hopes that St. Nicholas would soon be—

Goddammit, you've done it again. You can't let this keep happening. Get focused, nose to the grindstone (illegitimi non carborundum notwithstanding). Let it go, get back on track, rubber to the road, pedal to the metal, big wheels turning...

One wheel always fell off after hitting the rock in the road, shown in close-up just near the cliff, when the black hats wanting to rob the gold shipment were hightailing it closer on their galloping horses and firing off their six-shooters, while the stagecoach slewed to cliffside and you got the shot of the pretty maid virginal and fair, her white-gloved hand clutching a window frame as she swooned, the back of her other hand shielding her forehead to convey her distress. The stagecoach, now seriously swaying, perilously close to the cliff's edge, with dust rising from its dragging axle, while the driver cracks his bullwhip over the team of crazy-eyed horses and the hombre riding shotgun fires his Winchester and the black hats take aim (godsends of godsends were missing), as out of the sagebrush flashes White Hat on his trusty steed, galloping up beside the coach to leap from the saddle, cling to the door of the madly slewing coach, one boot on the footstep to grab the door, swing it wide (and miracle of miracles with striding danger music on edge-of-your-seat tension), take Missy in his strong arms, swing out to the still-racing-alongside Lucky, Trigger, Silver and rush beside the now-seriously-swerving stagecoach, to jump with the damsel now a flutter of white petticoats, layered underthings, and billowing dress, her legs waving in dainty orchid-like surrender, and with evident relief (the perfect O of her kiss lips), Lash LaRue sets her on his saddle horn—

Dammit all! Get with the program. How many times do you have to be told, for Chrissake...?

You trudge the riff of streets in a helmeted diving suit with lead belt and boots submerged in the murky waters of your own silent world with never a slip of the tongue, never a word overheard, an opinion expressed, not even a rolling of the eyes, but stiff upper lip of the brittle laugh and tight smile, while some clenching hand pinched your lifeline, you gasp, struggle, get your head above water, find yourself alone, explore solitary pursuits, pretend it isn't so: tell tales, grand whoppers, juggle, dazzle your audience, live two inches behind your face, visit your small-town museum: stuffed wildlife, arrowheads, empty British biscuit tins, the pioneer library: where a stark photograph under which no line of description, placement, no who, when, and especially why slipped between the pages of this random book in a wall of books, holding within its leaves a must of long-dead candles, eau de cologne, cigarette smoke, still holding the scent of the bibliographic search for a nugget, a motherlode held between their covers, where this one photograph slipped shilly-shally to the floor, to land by your feet and possess enough stark nakedness in its dead pictorial to root you to the spot, with enough curiosity seasoned with bewilderment to bend down and pick it up: the family plot…down the hill to the old part of the cemetery, under the ponderosa pines whose dropped needles formed an interwoven carpet leached of their green, to lay a rust-red layer over the entire plot-sectioned hillside, and searched for the plots where lay grandparents, parents, and the empty ground awaiting your arrival, where the now-dead bridal bouquet placed at the base of the marker by your spinster aunt, who was commonly referred to as "Poor Joan," lay…

They are here… You've been waiting, expecting, looking forward to the relatives…walking down from the driveway between the house and the Chinese elm hedge onto the expanse of lawn that leads down to the lake. Coming around the side of the house, excited and a little uncertain, to see who is on the lawn, already knowing by whose cars were in the drive, unsure perhaps of their greetings in the rush of feelings and memories brought into play by the anticipation of everybody gathering, until they are spotted or called out to, a long "Heeey!" And everyone in the lawn chairs jumps up, "They're here, they're here. Look who's here!" and, running around the chairs, bolts across the lawn as the new arrivals also run, to crash mid-lawn in a flailing of legs, arms, embraces and kisses, with a rush of "How was the traffic?" "I bet you're exhausted." "We just arrived." "Ruby, you look great." "Oh, Margaret! Come and sit… Beatrice… Elizabeth." "So, Ed, make your first million?" "Working on the second…" "Good to see you, Matt." "Heeey, Vic! Looking good." "Yeah, me and my spare tire." Beer suitcases shift from right hand to left for handshakes. Everybody in the shake-and-jitter dance people do when excited, shoulders this way and that, little jumps and two-step manoeuvres, hand wavings, grinnings, wide eyes, and serious momentary looks before a spray and explosion of laughter with the head tilted backwards, upward, so the spray showers into the sky until the heads come down with more banter and laughter. The gaggle moves over to the lawn chairs with "What'll you have?" Pairings take place as they sit, excitedly slip-sliding their bums this way and that in an endeavour to get closer, crossing their legs and unfolding them as they converse, especially the sisters. The men go off to unload cars or to the kitchen to mix drinks, and finally assemble under the acacia, their backs turned outward, staring intently into the centre of the circle where one is talking, until they all lean back in a roar of laughter, hoots spraying up into the acacia, while the sisters in the circle of lawn chairs rest their drinks in their laps or, extended arms resting on armrests, swirl their glasses to tinkle ice as they chat, laugh, lean close to one another in shared sisters' secret moments of cross-looks and crosstalk, prelude and overture to the disordered, dishevelled, and disarrayed hopes and plans in the intimacy of the kitchen.

She stands in the corner
garden in Her Sunday
best wearing an adorable
up-brim straw hat tied
with a bow in front of a
border of full-bloom tulips
where a birdbath statue
stands behind while Her
gaze averts right from
the probe of the camera

And below the circle of lawn chairs across the outstretch of lawn, its emerald flanked by flowerbeds with loopy lupines coming on where the eye travels down the levels to the beach while the lake wavers clips of silver across its chop, the lake, groundswell to the comings and goings, from winter skate to summer swim, or in darker moods wells up in rollers and whitecaps to crash over boathouse and pier, make puny our attempts to tame it but for a storm sail where main and jib sheets winched tight sing in the soughing of the wind bite, water racing down her gunwales as you thread your sloop into the maw of the storm, hand on the tiller, eye to the tell-tails, the belly of her sails hail and hearty to so ride the wind like kings, the lake rising in dreams, soft swells of endless summer or tempest tossed after ice comes off, its tempering of days and nights, its wash of green or grey, wave lap and winter nap waiting for its liquid spring and the long-looked forward view from a summer ring of chairs on the lawn, the lake where you are brushed, washed, bathed, and held in its amniotic centring still.

*

Margaret marshals the forces, with the men bringing out the big outdoor table and lighting up the barbecues, with Matt (the expert) taking the helm. Ruby and Beatrice organize dessert, bringing out date cakes, Nanaimo bars, and fruit crumbles, home-baked. Poor Joan directs the cousins to the dozens of cobs of corn and holds a shucking party, inspects the cobs to make sure all the silk has been removed while a few more brown-bagged bottles make their way into the kitchen, with little jokes like "Here's more fuel"... Hard stuff stashed in cupboards and beer in the guest-house fridge, with a case or two dumped into a Coca-Cola ice chest set over by the flowerbeds near the poplars and on the pathway up and down to the beach for convenience. Elizabeth has brought several towel-wrapped bottles of champagne all the way from California, along with Poor Joan's oversized jugs of booze, plus complaints about governments, taxes, and the high cost of mix. Aunts, uncles, cousins move to and from the kitchen out onto the lawn and the circle of lawn chairs with drinks before being called for the first meal, while cousins hurry to the beach after the shuck-up with whoops, jump, cannonball, sailor-dive, and bellyflop from the end of the pier, until with a slap from the back screen door Uncle Vic appears blindingly white, untouched by sun ray, wearing a bathing suit so brief, so tight as to show off his pathetic phalussy, and begins to sprint across the lawn with a hop skip jump, not quite natty around the circle of lawn chairs, his intention clear, ignoring shouts that "it's low water this year, don't dive!" his white streak even more horrendous against the green of the lawn, scampers down the ramp leading to the beach, hops onto the pier, and miles a minute down its length, ignoring the "Don't dive, don't dive," and swans off, arcing out over the water and splashing in while cousins wide-eyed know the outcome, watch as his legs wave slightly in the air as he hits bottom, stay there waving for a few seconds as they submerge, only to see Vic stand up with mud sliding off his chrome-dome, eyes bulging in the recognition that his Tarzan escapade has ended in another fuck-up, as cousins bend their knees to hide their laughter below the water but for telltale bubbles.

The best place to be was in the kitchen
when there was a get-together

With a plum tint overtaking the sky and a small onshore breeze to rustle leaves, it's time to think of dinner: And with a start and a look at their watches, gather up, looking left and right for plates, glasses, cigarettes, jump to it and gaggle across the lawn toward the kitchen to prepare dinner, leaving their presence in the empty bum-dimpled canvas seats of a circle of lawn chairs overlooking the lake view, framed by two willows between which the dark green water lies. And there in the kitchen, with openings of fridge, oven, cupboards, and the banging of pots, murmurs and cross-looks become whispers, intimate secrets hinted at, bubbling wavelets to ruffle just under the cooking and the laughter grown quiet: you'd sit and wait, out of the way, by the window, wait for the wave crests that would eventually wash at your ankles, then to your knees.

And there it was as it always was, just under a breath: "Poor Joan..."

She'd decided to walk the long way round, up and over First Hill and then down home, coming to the sun side where some farmer grew a patch of watermelons, and arrived home bloody in her torn dress. Shock waves smothered by the descending wet blanket of sexual silence held in the ring bond between sisters, and the three proposed trips to the altar broken, evaporated, colitis and vodka, "Poor Joan..."

The women, those sisters with shot glasses of rye and cigarettes: whisking batter into cake tins, strong-arming bowls of mashed potatoes, plating hot cobs, buttering homemade bread, arranging veg, heaving the roast out of the oven with frayed, burnt oven mitts, the right mixture of fat to flour, arranging fruit crumble, date squares, brownies, Nanaimo bars on the fancy plates from the china cabinet, sectioning fruit pies, peach, apple, rhubarb... And the men under the acacia: carburetors, gas mileage, winter tires, heroes of their own stories of deals and bargains, how to remove oil filters, what about that new tax?, who you gonna vote for?, did you get that raise?, smokin' a pipe now, eh?, watch you don't fall off and hurt yourself... In the circle under the acacia, Al up for a refill, looks bullet the circle, set mouths, hard eyes looking, the downward face of disappointment that whispered "alcoholic": the uncle who would leave his office, grab a twenty-sixer, get a cheap room on the bad side of town, toss the lid and take it straight... You imagine the bubbles jellyfishing upward through the tilted amber and are somehow afraid for him, imagine him sitting on the bed with his jacket off, loosened tie, his dark suspenders. Did he leave his hat on, tilt it back? You didn't know if he smiled or frowned, but something boiled up in you and you were afraid...

In Her first communion
dress with white veil
and knee socks She
stands at a corner gar-
den not quite smiling Her
eyes shadowed and be-
side Her a birdbath with
spiked lupines behind Her
in a garden of cupped
and outstretched tulips

A present cup-filled urge arises to place you at the crossroads, the fork in the road: the pinprick is arrival at a point of departure: time early or late, the right day, do you have your ticket, on what platform to stand, how long to wait, a decision to make: to climb aboard or not. You take the ride, settle into your seat, fasten your seat belt (could be forty miles of bad road), knowing full well, despite your evasions, diversions, art films, elite detective series from foreign parts, intense walkabouts in search of a ten-dollar lunch and the time suck, sharing with internetted groups, you will fail in this refined procrastination, this deferral inside a game of hide-and-seek, until finally disgusted at yourself, no longer able to shave in the mirror, resignedly kick the can, listen to its clatter across the road, until it comes to rest in the gutter by the sidewalk that borders the dry-grass boulevard, crumpled, battered, and pathetic...

They will ride by, white gloves bright in the dark rear window: snow-white teeth and those gloves perfectly cupped in slow motion, turning slightly, as the back of the hand rolls by: that's all there is, ever was, will be, allowing yourself to think about it, but quickly, before that seed thought grows into something too large, too tall, too unruly: snip it in the bud, give it a severe pruning, cut it off: you've got rent, a mortgage, a ring bundle of keys, an ass-flattened wallet, a deck of smokes, and standing at your knees: look down, look down a nest of open mouths...

You need to soar, swim-kicking for lift-off, fly above the quotidian: take off ascending, acrobatics, loop-the-loops, somersaults, daredevilish turnovers in your chicken-wire-and-canvas biplane, flying free from leg holds, obligatory knee bends, propelled escape past societies of handshakes pulling you into charmed circles, echelons of false exclusivities, black-kiss upgrades between the cheeks of ancient bifurcations, and you slip away in a smokescreen multicoloured for a moment's dazzling array to blind and obscure until you falter, fly too close to the sun, begin your burn, fall, crash, splinter, your wreckage landing in a box room, high-ceilinged, one high window you cannot reach, your fingernails scraped to the quick in the attempt to reach it, bread and water the highlight of your day, fevered escape plans reviewed, discarded, rewritten: high hopes a pinpoint held close, secreted in backwaters just under the surface of things, fevered antics to fool your jailers, phantom on a dim-lit stage, soliloquies, appeals, entreaties without audience, without bums in seats, unheard, unseen despite complimentary passes of no-shows, until you collapse in the far corner, a bundle of rags and stench, abject condition of your own unwashed spectre haunting nobody but yourself: you reach down, dip your hand below your surface of things, to bring up the near-dimmed coal of your almost forgotten red-ember pinpoint and begin to blow, to watch its glow light your face, feel its dry warmth reflected in your eyes, to see, in its burn, shades of your release if you choose, as the hero of your own story, the right door where lies the ancient casket waiting to be opened by the grip-touch of your very own hand...

It wasn't some hard-defined block of marble wherein lies the handsome boy...

Where you could intuit some line of beauty with your sharp chisel but formless, squishy, the kind when grabbed squeezed like shaving cream between your fingers: what others saw as expertise was really you not doing enough. You could do better, this is never right, more and more you told yourself, wondering when the blade would come down, slice to expose your interior: all cheap tricks performed on a sawdust floor, a rolling bandwagon, a manufactured hit from a carefully groomed boy band on the casting couch: RAZZLE & DAZZLE air-brushed into existence by blowing on the smouldering coal to heat the fork where the once-dormant lie, quickened into stirring, to be encoded, directed high road and low, but mostly low...

You stood there, soft, willowy: bent to the wind, north south east west, pressure systems, storm fronts, rolling thunder, a sunflower: stretching in the heat, head down, bent to let the wind blow over as you looked up, parted the present curtain, to reveal the tunnel where the steps you'd take would echo off the walls toward the far-end circle: one by one, the footfalls until you began to run: cringed, exercised, hollow, alone: what plan, distraction, divertimento, to step aside on the banks of the flow, to not quite engage, fool yourself: until on the pillow, quiet, accustomed to night sounds, between sleep and wake in the very zone you think you've placed yourself: streets you've strolled, quick-stepped, run down into, become the map you've so carefully quietly planned...

Introductions, meetings, greetings: traditions of courtly love from rough cuts to epicurean well-done, rare, *au point bleu*, first catch of the eye, arranged meeting, a song of love, an occasion of heart under the sill, a petitioning, an arrangement set from another order, a bit short-cut when you caught the eye: it was now, urgent, quick in a recessed doorway, up dark stairs, a place secure, no gatekeepers, no snoopy neighbours, to be able to come and go: flash of match light in a late-night park, drawn to the flame with fire alight, rough, quick, hot, and burnt, quiet, silent embers of an afterglow, at rest, of surcease, of occasion stolen constructed layer upon layer: RAZZLE & DAZZLE or, better still, DIRTY & THE DERELICTS—

"I want it
you got it
give it me"

A slide to make you feel good, desirous, left wanting for what has no name, bottoms up, there must have been a before before, you can only surmise, speculate, until you met another and it did not matter:

"I spy with my little eye
the wink from a piece of pie
O meo myo"

You called them Saturday songs: not rock 'n' roll hits, but songs you cherish, summer places held close, secret songs, you told nobody, kept them to yourself to keep the brood away, prevent their poking fingers if they knew too much: what you desire, what you love, need, badgered by their voices, held up to be seen, laughed at: the softness of those ballads you floated out on: you'd wear your clothes to bed on Friday night, place your shoes beside the bed, leave your coat next to the back door: come early Saturday, peel back the covers, slip into your shoes, grab the jacket slouched beside the door, and carefully, noiselessly, slip out, sneak along the side of the house and up the driveway to the fence of Douglas firs and into the gravel lane: clumps of chokecherries, spined leaves of Oregon grape, white snowberries against the green (and to the left, on their posts, the Queen's rural mailboxes you threw cannon busters into, to watch them rock back and forth, their lids flapping in their tin-can explosion, the air cut with gunpowder) to the end of the lane: you pry apart the barbed-wire strands to not get hooked and, ever so carefully, so as not to get your shoes wet, step along the clumps of grass and weed through the marsh reeds, bulrushes, dark pools and rivulets, to the small pebble-strewn beach, hidden by willows, and listen to the calls of red-winged blackbirds, to be alone, gloriously alone, before the world wakes up...

You arrive at your front door, again, full circle as you knew you would, hide-and-seek, the kick of the can: come unwanted, out of place, un-invited into the dining room, the studio, your bedroom, found in your chest of drawers, on the bedside table, in the backpack in the closet waiting for you to find it, the rust that never sleeps, keeps you awake, scratches across your dreams: untidy reminder

la vie en rose
la vida rosada
the pink life

O meo myo of pity politics, let's collect one more injustice, have a pro-test, *una manifestación*: we'll carry placards, get marching, bogeymen at the top of the stairs, the ones your mother told you about, the butt of jokes *(He hit me with his purse full of quarters!)*, fagots on fire to burn the faggot, to purify his body, to release his soul in the uplifting smoke, his screams one grand spectacle.

Who knows when: you started out, came out, got brought out, taught the confections: spun sugar, cotton candy, jujubes, fruit gums, and those pubescent dreams: walking in the sand-ochre desert to come upon a gigantic book of paper matches: so tall, long, upright, the flare of their red heads as you stood looking up, way up: or all those tadpoles with horrified faces clawing up the toilet bowl as you flush: you insist, persist, keep bringing them up and letting them drown...

From the start: mendicant, supplicant on bended knees, scrapes, lances, hearts with holes, wounds, thorns, *ora pro nobis*: intervene, make way, intercede: a go-between, panderer, and pimp: a stash you can't have, don't own, made poor, stained, a blotch, a dropped key: the we, the you, the them pontificating: a club where you have no name, where the doorman asks, "You have papers?"

Here they are, you drop your drawers: unclenched bifurcations award the trope of the midnight raid, *Open sesame* to the dark cavern where the treasure trove of pearl, ruby, sapphire overflowing awaits to be plucked, pocketed, secreted in warm, sweated folds in the deep end with a slow incursion, initial gasps, succumbing, willing, wanting precisely this: special moves, a variety of styles, intertwinings, reach-arounds, slip slides, heat waves ascending, rising from beds, cots, couches, from late-night parks environmentally safe as the city slept, returning to copses, hedgerows, off beaten paths, in thickets, manly spatters, leaves, carpets of moss, in arboreals, evergreen and deciduous, floating upward, ascending to heaven to form vapour trails among the cumulus, cloud towns in white flotillas across the blue, to reach the Milky Way...over the rainbow, far, far away...

But you're in a bad way, you need help: you limp up the hill, puff to the top, drag ass across the road, fall flat at the set of steps you must climb, crawl up one by one, arrive at the great door, lay your weakened shoulder to the wheel (excuse me, the door): it squeaks aside, you hit the carpet, lizard up the aisle: there is a rail, a cream separator dividing you, penitent, from the swish of gold-threaded robes, incense clouds the air, wine is poured, bread wafers handed out: you're invisible, no one sees you wave, hears your cry: turn from the hemorrhage that is your heart, you look like a roll of rags, you've hit your bottom, at the end of the road: things are stern despite the choir, bells, candlelight, incensed fumes reaching to the starlit nave: genuine gold stars on sky blue, here's heaven, pearly gates: search for your ticket, convinced of your reservation: no name on the clipboard, you might be taking the low road (like you've never been there before), you could duck your head, you do just in time:

Something's hit the fan, Stan
You're lookin' black, Jack
You're Indian red, Ned
You're a Nellie gay, Ray
There's a thousand ways
to apply the leverage
toke the smoke
booze the beverage
There's a thousand ways
to blow your lover

In all the while of your not knowing you have plied the Divertimento for One Hand, Opus 13, with baptismals of spit, holy chrism of lube, intimate fingerings, blessings spiced by the pure impure inching closer to finally, completely, drown in the soar of the only heaven you've ever known.

But you begin the most dangerous of things: pretend to yourself you can run away, hide away in daily things: cycles of dishes, laundry, food to replenish, purchase, stock up: it doesn't last for more than the first few sips: the wall you think you've built begins to crumble into the elements of its construction: blood, bone, sinew, and muscle to hide desire: you give up as you know you would, lay down your puny armour, raise your hands, fall in surrender, taken hostage and prisoner, marched off to the barbed-wire enclosure, that most dangerous place: chain-link of memory and desire...

Not that you let the cat out of the bag or anything: you've snuck out many times before, standing an inch or two behind your face, unnoticed in the crowd: when you rode a tricycle, the world rode bicycles, left you behind on Saturdays: you named them "summer songs," charmed summer places, spooky and sunny to the beat of a different drum in the wetlands at the end of the lane, goat-footing on clumps of grass in dark pools green with duckweed through reed beds, stands of bulrushes where red-winged blackbirds sing conk-la-ree, conk-la-ree in the grey morning between dark and light, you learned to hide and seek: you quick-stepped over the Rialto, knocked on the sculpted door knockers of Venice, with *chateaubriand* under the hideous fluorescents in La Luna where canals run seeping, sailed to the stone on sand in Crete, Ierapetra, where available men rolled marble gods along the road, bullet-pocked buildings along the Paseo Marítimo of old Malaga after a three-day shelling, scissoring across Bloor and Yonge, Georgia and Granville, scurrying with your beaver pelts in the wind bite of Portage and Main (but you stop for an artiste, who for a few coins will write your name in an ancient script you cannot read but admire for its coils and curlicues, a small souvenir you passed to a translator friend, to reassure yourself that your few miserable centimes were well spent, who prof-

fers his inestimable translation: "One born every minute, asshole!"),
up Cuesta del Chapiz across Calle Panaderos through Plaza Larga to
the Moorish arch to the Mirador (where you step into a recessed doorway to let pass a tourist herd following a purple umbrella, while trying
to decipher maps, which through a slight miscommunication with the
printer have been printed upside down yet retain small red dots to sig-
nify where you may meet a stranger in the night, exchanging glances,
what are the chances à la Frankie) and down the San Agustins, ending
at Chapiz and your own front door as you knew but hid, slid from a full
frontal, and you'd done it again, now forced to sit slightly blurred in
the antique mirror, to wrap yourself in the warm smells of that long-
ago kitchen, bread and fruit pie, cigarettes and rye, to revisit that soft,
silent, voiceless world but for the whisper of reeds, sway of bulrushes,
call-call-calling of red-winged blackbirds alit on the rushes, burble of
rivulets trickling into the wide-bodied lake: its mirrored sheet unwrin-
kled where the water blink of memories wring, wrench, and writhe of
women in the kitchen...

In full sun and colour She
stands in front of a caragana
hedge beside irises and pink
daisies wearing Her confirma-
tion white dress, and wide-
open smile hands in prayer
Her overexposed white posed
before backgrounds of green

And there they were…

Secrets come pouring, incidents, situations, horrors: He stole a wallet from our best friends / the tubal pregnancy almost killed her / found him on his hands and knees, licking up the rye from a broken bottle / he spilled hot tar on her / his handyman roof job / three weeks in the hospital / brought syphilis home from the army / got robbed by a prostitute in Las Vegas / at the bank party he called him a Bohunk / him standing there with that ridiculous pot of apricots to say he was sorry / blood transfusions gave her AIDS / who was talking about that then? / the plug had to be pulled / separate beds for the last twenty-five years / she asked him on her deathbed not to marry that woman / she took the money and threw out the wedding dishes / the last child almost killed her / borrowed twenty thousand for the wedding and refused to pay his brother back / lost the lake house to gambling debts / the adopted one with the rotted teeth a born-again / the natural one wanted for murder / God knows where he is / she had a lot of acquaintances but no friends / Christmas gifts all wrapped up but none in return / they should have divorced / the Monsignor said it was okay to take them after the last one / the baby daughter and those men, those men She brought home / the bank called about the massive overspending on Her credit card / the private detective hired to find Her and send Her home from Hawaii / three weeks past Her two-week holiday.

… What you know and what yet you do not know you know, to finally, quietly, sit to let drain these secrets from the tips of your fingers, from the tips of your toes, to be in solitude, to be outside this point of time, to breathe without other voices, this dawning, this red morning: Hey, sailor…take that warning!

The sailor and his sloop

You want out but don't know where on the run of a lifeline, finger down, a point or pin, a before and after, from both sides of your mouth, stretch your arms east west north and south, from the perfectly ordered garden of loopy lupines and brown-eyed Susans, between the cascade of two weeping willows framing the linear, square, rectangular, and circular gardens, where you forage and rummage, poke, dig, and grub, pick up the trail in a darker landscape of a forest too silent to be real: trailblazing through bush, around muskeg, swamp, alkaline pond, across grasslands where you're the only thing spotted above knee height but for the poplars shielded in the coulees gathered close on hills at the end of the night, day taken its pound to what crowds in, niggling undone bits, untoward things bump and grind, to shield with your arms, to shut your eyes, turn off your head, flat upon your bed at the end of the night, no sleep, again...

You have upright breathing, beating heart: you look out, start walking toward what unwinding you do not know: pick them up, put them down on what is named path, journey, exploration: following what exactly? Perhaps not unwinding but winding, answering a call, the call the question of forward progression: sailboating: setting, trimming, hauling jib and mainsheets, close to the wind, to beat, reach, wing on wing, surge and corkscrew, make waves, box your compass, set your course: buffeting headwinds in the direction you want to travel, destination you think you know but really merely want: aware of the ever-present possibility of storm, black clouds, wind force, wave action, current drift, tide levels with your hand on the tiller, standing to windward, false dominion over your intended command, eyes shielded under your visor for rocks awash: telltale white foam alit in dark water, assured of your passage, furled, unfurled: sharp white triangles wind-bellied, conceived of wind:

sailor, sailor, captain of your ship...all you survey from your sloop...
read from the face turned to the wind, smooth, smiling, polite: never
any trouble nor a ripple to wrinkle the surface of things, solid middle
class with amenities, you looked back, review circumstantials: you want
to skate, glide, fly, soar with violins, troop with brass, flutter with wood-
winds, sip the first remove from the daily press, slip into a mood where
whispers flex: to chamfer the edges of the day: abrasions, jokes to con-
ceal pinpricks, mutters, eyes that slide away, wary of words that may of-
fend delicate feelings, negotiating on tiptoe, eggshells decorously placed
on sidewalks, paths, alleyways, streets of what was at a time long before
hometown turf, harbours from distant lands, huts, brutal apartments,
erupted streets, shell-shocked cities with ways and means never encoun-
tered, and in innocence cannot imagine agendas, ploys, subterfuges,
manipulative skills, shell games of the shuffling cards to keep your eye off
the ball for sleep, well-deserved rest at the switch, where on the nod you
finally fall fast to the ever-present tape loop, a reminder of your diver-
sionary saltings, phony invoices, cash under the table, *dinero negro*, pale in
the light of what you really want...what you know, what you need... Good
ground to throw out your anchor, safe harbour, moorage, bow, stern
and spring lines clove-hitched, bright work polished, shipshape in Bris-
tol fashion, looking good for a first review, welcome aboard, a nest in the
fore peak, wave-lapped to sleep, a gentle swell, a rocking to and fro, wave
rock and tide rip for the oncoming tsunami for which you are prepared
with flotation device and life ring to be saved from dark waters, buoyant,
outstretched arms of deckhands pulling you to safety, safe in their arms,
tender embraces, warmth given, warmth taken, revivifying mouth-to-
mouth resuscitations, deep breathing, swelling of your chest, blood flow
in spongiform parts for an appreciated resurrectional, a ménage à trois,
Neptune's trident: sea wrack, seafoam, sea tang with shanties: "Yo-ho-
ho and a throttle of bum."

Oh Puck, it's you again

Camped for the night, starless, moonless, anxious for a prodigious shaft of sunlight to push the arboreal aside, make clearing, where *coureurs de bois*, shirtless, welcome, with upraised arms, warmth. The arboreal neither silent nor deaf for those bivouacked under deciduous coniferous, beside pond, creek, and river flow: scratchings, burrowings, rustlings, bat wing and hoof beat and the breathing of leaves, ground, root, and night cries of flesh punctured by fangs and the morning's evidence of blood, bone, and fur.

Perusing menus: swimmer's body, hairy bear, boy next door, leather, rubber, elfin cutie, gym built, bottom up top down: I saw you on my phone, we can meet, four streets away, on a block near you, an ass that won't quit, there's something for you, get your GPS on, buy the app, we'll connect, don't be afraid, find your mate: I'm late, I'm late for a very important date, down the rabid hole where you kneel at the altar with your hands spread for the propped-up vertical crescent of the eager bifurcation slowly advancing to your flushed face, a Chaucerian smote to meet ring to ring, rictus to rictus, black kiss and the blowback of poppered breath amidst the rising now writhing moons poker-waiting for the heat verge and the after drink of water, water everywhere nor any drop... The weighty dead albatross of a chance meeting, hope springing as he walks out on the springboard, two bounces for lift-off with a one-and-a-half gainer, to slip into the pool with hardly a ripple, opening his eyes into the surrounding aqua, embryonic, warm, cosseted, to re-emerge glistened wet, a medallist sculpted in ancient gymnasia, accepting offers to star in *Swimmer in the Wild*, where hiking in the deep arboreal, relaxing in a sunlit clearing, he sunbathes, oblivious to the stealthy parting of nearby bushes, where a duo of *coureurs de bois* rush to assail this offering, lucky that a cameraman happens to be available to point his trusty lens into the heart of a series of ongoing intimacies, thrusts, openings where after they agree to meet in the city, where product placements of red jockstraps, particular lubes for the necessary passages, expensive patterned sheets on a king-sized bed above which hang carefully positioned abstracts in pleasing colour patterns modelled for eager DVD buyers who could own the same in a pathetic case of sympathetic magic, until the next fantastical round-up necessitating a call to the local decorator for yet another redo occurs.

He pushes you against the deciduous you embrace, reaches around, undoes your belt, unzips with one pull now resting at your ankles, and with a sigh synaptic electric you fall, succumb to what you've known all along, you present yourself, you feel his smile on your back, hear his zipper, there snapping, caressing up your now eager…his agile expertise makes your whole wide world turn on his axis, a star, your…ass is a star!

Erected on the tent pole that supports pyramidal shelters of voyageurs in the deep arboreal, sheathed from the depredations of inclement weather patterns: rain, snow, sleet, wind gusts threatening to pull out your stakes, expose your nakedness to the pinpricks of a million stars and a big fat moon reflected from your white pale but happy bifurcated marshmallows, while Puck presents, controls the action beneath you: pert palpitations, butterfly flutterings, rocks and rolls: joyful exaltations echo, ricochet, wrap round, whip through gullies over hills, climb mountains, melt snow and glacier forming freshets foaming white water, pure white water in which you cup your hand to slake your thirst, wash your parts, refresh your face, and in the depth of your eyes reflect how bottomless, deep, and profound, Puck's inestimable charms meet your gaze, shape-shifting bottom who can make your day with words in your mouth.

Ringing the bell

Ringing the bell, a couple modestly, evangelically dressed, he in a cheap suit, she a homemade dress up to her neck, offer pamphlets, scripture cards, and a monthly journal of admonishments and finger-wagging, until they are told Catholics live here, prompting grave looks, concerns, a question: "Have you been abused?" the front door firmly closing, slamming, while the question hangs in mid-air, somersaults, flies on the trapeze, a three-legged race, the shuffling audience struck dumb (**"Do not mention absolutely anything at all!"**): traipsing to private bedrooms to change from Sunday best into the slouch of casual, comfortable, well-worn clothes, camouflage to divert attention from any possible detail that might attract surveillance, unwanted probings, surreptitious intelligence gatherings, wiretaps into thought, feeling, patterns of survival, dynamics familial and otherwise, that would delve into the calamity at the front door...

Not so strong and free

A space, an opening where you tread water, float, begin to swim free
of your immersion in the quotidian between the cup of wine, the flute
of champagne (never a drink too far to be heightened), lifted, to enter
a clarity of memory, dread memory of things said, things not done, of
long-forgotten incidents buried in the flotsam and jetsam you juggle
to keep the wary eye averted, entertained by tumbling and gymnastic
freaks, the Bearded Lady and the Alligator Boy, scenes you've hardly
revealed to yourself, now presented in a spectacular array in the trape-
zia of your convoluted cortex, grey matter, swarming maggoty interdic-
tions, commandments, no-nos of hard eyes, pointed fingers (**"Bless
me, Father, for I have—" "Not again, you little turd!"**). O, the Jesu-
itical enwrappings, inculcations, fought-fors in the muddy trenches of
your urinating, defecating, perspiring, and sperming body, its halitosis
of reek where all the bathwater, the anointed bathwater, locked in the
cistern where the soap is for sale if you fall to your knees to open the
O of your mouth to the salvatory member for a communion of milk
to replace the nourishment of the Blessed's immaculate teat, with glad
tidings of a job well done, Halleluiahs from the princes of piece, S&M'd
in a good and necessary flagellation of the oh so impure that you are...
"Bring it on," you've felt the experienced hands, helping hands of a
fellow voyageur, a Radisson and des Groseilliers penetrating the deep
arboreal, traversing muskeg and swamp, stepping lightly over millen-
nia of coniferous needles, deciduous leaves, portaging around spills of
whitewater, shooting in your trusty *bateau* your *canots du nord*, your *canots
du maître* over rapids, log jams, boulders, swatting dreaded blackflies
and mosquitoes, while stinking of bear grease and comfortable fart-
ings (efficacy of pine cone tea), hoping, expecting, wanting refuge in a
clearing of the woods and nightly rest with well-worn woodies and the

intolerable waiting for a soft spot of heat to nullify chilly evenings with the ascending sparks of your frail fire: in the glowing eyes of red embers imagine the invention of marshmallows, wieners, hot dogs, with which you berate yourself for their jiggery pokery, their nighttime insistence, until with sly looks and shy glances you assess the possibilities of an infringement, a little touch-up, a bushwhack, and with another half-day trek, come upon, blessedly, Airstream trailers circled round a firepit where roasts *entrecôte de buffalo* with bowls of pemmican set aside and slavering, mouth watering, stomach grumbling, hastily run to the movable feast before it moves, with humble apology for your complete lack of manners, until satiated, belly full, you burp and belch into a gratified yet dreamful stupor nor heedless of the impure demands beginning to well in the interstices, synapses, tingling bits, and gush of blood flow in spongiform parts and a pitter-patter of tiny deer feet turning goat-footed...a provisioning of victuals for the back country... (**"Oh no, not the back country!"**)

You know this, understand this from months of research at Archives Canada, now irreparably digital, losing texture of paper, colour of ink, collated traceries of networks of authorial friendships, crossovers, meetings, having purchased notebooks from the paper dealers and sellers of fine editions in Montreal and Muddy York for those voyageurs on the hunt for beaver (animal and otherwise, or if in a pinch...), who may be found building, writing, plotting their journeys and wanderings in the arboreal with journals kept safe from the travails of whitewater, burning bush, outright thievery and espionage by rival corporate fur traders, to be held for future reading, investigation, and the bolstering of thematic papers with supportive footnoting, indexing, and referencing irrefutable: when in your search for that nugget, that perfect letter or journal that would reveal all unknowns and secure your tenure in the halls and towers, ivory or not, of academe, the gods of literary endeavours smiled, blessed, and allowed a buckskin-bound notebook to fall from the near-rotted slipcase with such a satisfying plop beside your shoe, you could not help but bend to pick it up and, riffling through its pages, came upon this… Well, you didn't know what to say or call it, but as you followed along the cursive, a frisson of tumescence enraptured both your body and mind.

But would you dare do so… It's publish or perish, sweetie, knuckle down!

Handsome Huritt

There was a breathing tenderness and beauty
in the sleeping boy that seemed to send forth
sweetness. In the boys' playful eagerness they
half tore off his buckskin vest before he was
aware. He awoke in time, however, to escape
from their busy hands tugging at his breech-
cloth, but enough of his charms had been revealed to convince Black Robe that they were
not to be rivalled. From this day on, the heart
of Black Robe was inflamed. He gazed on the
beautiful Huritt with fervid desire and sought
to read in his looks whether there was levi-
ty or wantonness in his demeanour, but the
eye of the boy ever sank beneath his gaze, and
remained bent on the earth in shyness and
modesty. Being one afternoon in the woods
where the boys were diverting themselves,
and coming to the pond where he had beheld
the innocent boys at their sport, he could no
longer restrain the passion that raged within
his breast. Seating himself beside the pond,
he called Huritt to him to draw forth a thorn
that had pierced his hand. The boy knelt at his
feet to examine his hand, and the touch of his
slender fingers thrilled through his veins. As
he knelt, too, his dark locks fell rich about his
beautiful head, his innocent bare chest pal-
pitated, and his timid blushes increased the

effulgence of his charms. Having examined Black Robe's hand in vain, he leaned up in his face with artless perplexity.

"I can find no thorn, nor any sign of wound," said he.

Black Robe grasped his hand and pressed it to his heart. "It is here, handsome Huritt!" said he. "It is here, and thou alone canst pluck it forth!"

"Niyaw!" exclaimed the blushing and astonished boy.

"Huritt!" said Black Robe. "Dost thou love me? Let us repair to a secret thicket where I may bestow—nay, offer—my swart brute verge into the portal of your charms to quell my hirsute desires in the way of the one true God."

Huritt rose from the earth where he had hitherto knelt, his soft eye kindled at these words. "I can receive no dignity from such vile means... Black Robe, you propose violence."

Questions tennis-ball in the forecourt of your lobes, considerations of right and left, negotiations, fence-sitters pulled in every direction: there would be parsings, gender equations, appropriations to be tiptoed around, across, and over, hidden agendas with leg-hold traps, pitfalls, quicksands all so carefully negotiated, grumblings in exclusive clubs, plans made to discredit your endeavours, the quick pull of the rug on which you stand... Can you hold your ground, what will this bring, at once gift and penalty, but these are not all the arrows penetrating, piercing, slung into the body of you and your research, but the frisson of tension of what may be discovered of your own involvements, secrets, furtive escapades, couplings, your own jiggery pokery: you, the mayor of teen town, trolling for rent boys in your invisible black robe, reeling in that smooth brown Aboriginal boy, Gabriel the angel, a star, a northern light, a wounded Huritt who for a negotiated sum performed, enacted, rehearsed yet again the original conditions of his abuse, the generational effect transmitted across the survivors of deafening silence racked in the residential jails of betrayed intimacies, probings, under the criss-crossed Christ, deaf pleadings to be held close, to be warmed, to be loved... What will you do with the recognition of your agency, complicity, culpability, but kneel before him to proffer hopeful expiation, mumbling, gagging, dripping spit...where wanton memories stumble, fall slack-jawed, while your bootless cries rise in the temporal of your self-inflicted and outrageously pathetic fortune, crippled and gimped within yourself...

You need, you search to find, a way out of this deep quotidian, find yourself in the dark wood. You step toe-heel across a bed of rust-red pine needles, careful not to slip on dropped cones of Ponderosa pines oozing gobs of pitch scenting the air, to find the clearing you've heard about, whispered and mythic. Is this actual? Does the dark glade exist? You think of the abstract expressionist painter charging down the length of his studio, armed only with brushes and colour (and chocolate syrup for a descent into the frivolities of dessert and another flute of champagne) with which to enact an action painting, an event to defy the daily press, to gesture significant from the platform of Western philosophies of individualism in the face of anonymity and the degradations of uncivil world war. Where the kinder in the garden born under good omens, bode wells, portentous auguries is hidden, switched and raised by good, common, blue-collar folks in the Airstream trailer in the deep woods, rises by means of a hard scrabble: hoarding cash, buccaneering raids, arm twists and backslaps, calculating layers of obligation, smoothing the voice, polishing the come-on, gesturing swiftly across genitals and buttocks to meet the challenge of choosing the right door, the appropriate box, gold silver bronze or red white blue, or between a Giller-nominated book, a cultural donation in his name, or an envelope bulged with cash. He chooses the cash to solve the riddle (as arranged by members of the club), to engage in mortal (to him it's always mortal) combat with a corporate dragon, a financial minotaur, but never himself to become victorious over perceived evil forces and the ambitious machinations of corporate raiders, hedge-fund liquidators, to be recognized for his high and noble birth now enriched with liquid capital in the throne room in the court of the high condo penthouse for an inestimable photo shoot (displayed in the rags at checkout), to mask his place on the great white throne where steamed vapours arise from his refined paste containing high nutritional content as reminder of his own immediately forgettable corruption with well-fed flatulence (an ill wind blows no good) and comfortable sins...

You can't stand it anymore, you don't want to hear them, no longer want to listen: those false royals supported by a host of thousands to not be who they are, makeup artists with years of training to airbrush you out, make you an image, lighting experts who know the advantages of cast light and withheld shade on the *tabula rasa* of a face, oiling their way to finger in the place where you want at the centre of things: we are desired to own it, you know the place, the most powerful one that rips your system, setting nerve end to synapse with St. Elmo's fire, forked lightning that cracks you open, makes you thunder, its seepage, its horrendous manipulation, buttons to press to finally finish at the finished line, broken tape, better than you could ever own, yet still that place: its G spot, its sore spot: your most wide open, your entry into the delicious hand-wringing between need and want: the things you do when you rut, when the sniffing and licking begins, when the pink comes out: the dance when the endearments win, while the violence of financials wends its weary-making way to jailbait the impulses under the surface of things to finally shrug down, slink into the cave of yourself, pull your tentacles in, and wait in the gloom to fire your light under your bushel basket, or bask in the sun in your own beachfront lounge, to consider the relationships of cabbages and kings: chains of your governance for the haves and the noughts to pay out the string of your time, slow reduction of your ball of twine, to consider the splitting of hair, its shave by the blade, its razor in time, to gain some lift-off and sadly rise to the pockmarked sublime in a course of withdrawal from the engagements with your so precious, so star-studded, so knotted time...

The beloved buyer

You wake up hungry. It's cold. You need breakfast. You dash
stomach-grumbling to your local franchise. You slide up to an
available cashier who greets you:
"Good morning, what'll you have."
"G'morning, an oatmeal, please."
"What size?"
"Just oatmeal."
"There must be a size."
"No, just an oatmeal."
His fingers hover over the order pad.
You turn to the next cashier and say, "Oatmeal."
He turns to your cashier and says, "Oatmeal."
Your cashier says, "Oatmeal."
You say, "Oatmeal."

And the pitchmen come…

Where what went when you wouldn't ask any more sidling up close to the closed door you dare not pry open with things being comfortable, just enough, as hemmed by the repetitive cycle of what bad guys get because they all get got, which could well be your end…

Same old when you decided on the movie, when those ones you'd been taught to fear were going to blow the stadium up just as the national anthem was in full throat, led by somebody winsome, before their voice cracked and goldarnit them cavalry just came charging over the hill in the nick of time, just the way the govmint didn't, but you so hoped they would and were told they did, while the whole theatre in an orgasmic throe of an arpeggio of bugle numbers and thundering hooves, helicopters, and tattered but still-flying flags carried by Tommy the Freckle Face running on the sugar high of apple pie and the picture of Missy next to the condom ring in his wallet, worried about the mortgage, car payments, and bills for another baby, hoofing the good fight up Bloodlust Hill and over to plant the flag-flap deep into vanquished territory, as the sunsets bootyful on the camaraderie of heart-warming tropes, dry as popcorn at a thousand per cent profit margin, along with an ice cube–laden soda to take up room for less Coke syrup, for another debit card grab on a night out and hoped-for relief from the existential tensions…

You never really know, but palm cuddle yourself with the assurance of cliché and trope that things will be fine and all will work out, until the nightmares arrive in colour-awakening night sweats: that rising up and out from the twist of sheets to call out to nobody in the dark bedroom. Horror of that headlong drive into speeding forward at ever-increasing momentums, while lateral vision becomes border blur without the sleep that gives rest in the eerie green light of screens, phones, connectivity of the whole wide world, right now accelerated with augmented tourism in your own body nomadic, travelling, driving, running madly in your body bag with even more speed down the supposed freeway...

You worry at night when the greenbelt gets cinched and the land laid out there between the windbreaks standing down the side road, squared fields rolling in the distance, rough with stumps of cut corn below the stand of a woodlot in late fall dusted with first snow, but out there in the arboreal, the silence of snow, the deafness of an erected god...

You fall back, sink to the floor, gulp for breath as this enormity, this grand plan of what can be taken as thesis for a peer-reviewed journal, this little book falling into your hands, from where, who wrote it, what it means: obvious blowback to these black-robed desires, fingerings, molestations, the whole edifice ripped open, internals exposed, this day's dead sanctities, a virus, a pox, a plague borne through the arboreal, winding its boned finger and pestilent breath into the intimacies that make you alive...

Efficacious therapy of a freshly cut wedge of wood: abundant species from our arboreal forests of coniferous and deciduous, each with the ineluctable taste while inserted with firmness and attention to detail, to remind the penitent speaker that his own inferior language, with its now bitter taste of lignin and acidic sap, will bond with the assertion (insertion) that the glorious expression of English-French will outpour from the mouth to rapturous vaultings of articulation and God-fearing joy...

Grey Owl

You'd leave 3607 Mara to walk down behind the big elementary school with the dome on top, where you'd file up from class to watch Grey Owl films. He'd walk out of Beaver Lodge and introduce you to his beaver kits, Rawhide and Jellyroll. Sometimes he took you down to the river ponds, where you could see their parents' lodge made of sticks they gnawed at night. Some shows flew you over the Great North, filmed from the cockpit of a de Havilland Beaver. You could hear the Pratt & Whitney cough, catch, and smooth out when the pilot gunned it, and see the float plane lift off the lake, tracing a water spray sparkling in sunlight over the forest that stretched to the horizon, where trees sawtoothed into the sky in black and white, the sound of the film travelling through the projector's sprockets just below some guy's voice-over, describing unlimited natural resources. North-end boys sitting in the back row joked about beaver, but you didn't understand.

Grey Owl, who visited the King and Queen in his buckskins, brought the gift of a dried beaver tail (which Her delighted Highness promptly used for paddling the bums of her unruly children; quoted as saying it left a nice criss-cross pattern—gossiped later in the *Daily Mirror* that Chuck employed the tail as an overture to his spongiform engagements). Meanwhile, back at the Montreal docks, Grey Owl arrives to a welcoming committee of schoolchildren waving handfuls of maple leaves and pine boughs, to be sent off in a waiting de Havilland Beaver, trailing watery diamonds from the St. Lawrence out over the dark green arboreal, sawtoothing into the far horizon, only to be kicked in the groin when the pilot sees no lake to land on, no ponds, no trickling rivulets nor creeks, the beds of lakes now dustbowls, and there among the coniferous stands a forlorn Beaver Lodge, high and dry. Grey Owl, now struck with the lightning that fires dry brush, comes to know that those God-be-damned fur traders and trappers have stolen the show and wrecked in twenty years a thousand years of water conservation, while Rawhide and Jellyroll are now hats in the fashionable streets of London and Paris, respectively, with a tip o' the hat in the hopes of finding a damsel in distress to prove their valorous ways in the inner city, far from the arboreal and the tiny screams of leg-trapped beavers. You are blown out of the water (dustbowl) when you find out Grey Owl was a British-born huckster (Archibald Belaney) with wives and children abandoned while he constructed a mask of Native heritage as slippery as the canoe he paddled through river reeds. Another poster-boy set-up you placed faith in as a picture of the True North Strong and Free, redemption, transformation of trapper to conservationist as false as unlimited natural resources, the whole thing built on the back of a rodent... Now what? You could dig deeper into biography and his own abandonment, the issues that never leave despite the geographical cure, which never helps but enables the act-out in the North, that place shouldered on the borderline of the south, the North that waits out there where Grey Owl eternally snowshoes through the stands of poplars and birch (where you enrol in the enlightenment, the understanding that this is the place of an acting-out, a frontier of lawlessness, without rules to introduce the white dick of rapacious desire, to impose, to usurp the names of ancient history, to supplant without understanding, not a moment of a deep breath in the dark wood that reveals another order, a way of the world that teaches reverence in the silent spaces between coniferous and deciduous, of travelling the ground on which you stand).

Grey Owl snowshoeing and exhausted, weighed down by the travois of his deceit, falls to his knees into the clearing to await the arrival of Sergeant Preston of the Yukon, "On, King! On, you huskies!" in the fading hope that Nelvana of the Northern Lights, travelling on the Aurora Borealis, will show the way, her arcing light, green and spiking into the sky brighter than the moon, radiant across lit diamonds of snow, will reveal the hidden trail that will take him away from the wind soughing through the arboreal night screams, patches of blood reddening the torn white fur, footpads leading into dark, still underbrush: impenetrable, silent, blanketed, broken by the lone howl of the wolf and the terror of the pack to which you he we belong.

A glimpse of the lake across the lawn to Her left while behind a riot of yellow flowers backgrounded by leafy trees She holds a large trophy with a smaller one to Her left Her long blond hair tied in tails She wears knee-high socks a yellow top with matched shorts She squints in the bright sun unsmiling head cocked Her face squelched

Look, don't touch

But you were a good boy on bended knee, hands folded, you'd completed a novena, stations of the cross: but something was missing, you could feel it without a name, your unanswered prayers to be guided: you needed a helping hand, the hand of God, a touch-up...lone-wolfing the turn of boy to man, a turn to the underhand...

Point where you begin the turning you didn't, the street you didn't, you wanted, you were stepping along, one foot in front of the other, just moving along one at a time, there you go, one more, you can do it, that's it, move along, you have your papers, very good, you have your rebellion, it's almost complete, you've gone some distance, see the horizon, is that sunrise or set, do you care right now, do you want to care right now or any now, really, have you thought about it, sat on the philosopher's log, head jammed against your closed fist in the position of the good, heavy elimination, the very fundament, just passing through, its metaphor in *potens*, which begs construction–constructor infighting to the point of silence but for unruly clamour heard before, but if you'd taken that other road, well, you know it's all been done, your addition, if you thought so big, was where at this point, being the point bearing down on another going, without plan, depending on rapier wit of the moment to carry somewhere, someplace, its mere insistence will break down the muffled maladroit lip movements, the synapse that fires brain wave into startling light of unperceived perception in some arrogant sense, gesture might make the direction of a communiqué out over telecasts, beat back for a sound bite emanating but briefly to part the overcast that clouds hanging over you of where what when you went and didn't, this sound like the same old entrapped in plot subject verb object plod that for the life of you unable to break out, asound the general alarm astounding from the watchtowers at the four corners under the klieg lights gen-pop busy with vaudeville routines, slapstick hoof numbers and the plates you had for dinner, nice 'n' neat all from round here in the radius, with definite hints of next morning's dumpable refinement and ever so friendly, you know how it is, just another level of exclusionary numbers high-kicking chorus line svelte, suave, saucy, the haughties all in a row and how does your nose grow with pretty smells all in a blow, back from pen to paper, type to screen effervescence of it and you in it rising on the ascending aflutter dispensary magnanimous kiss-blows, pert waves, stamping your little shoes, tantrum over the rainbow and a galaxy far, far away with big ears spouting philosophicals on which you are to be aboard on the flight deck, manhandling joysticks, reading the whirling dials, gauging wind drift, current drive, and overmatter scree formations, bad bumping forty miles of mean-street canyon riffs; the get-down-to doing down-low peregrinations, where rubber greets the load in the no-man's land, right up there in loin territory, the soft spot of the fork part and how wet to make it for another infancy grab, "We sellin' it, special like...from the inside of my overcoat, just pay my pal, who'll take the direction from where you're travelling and send you on your way in no-time flat out," out damn fly fleck spotting the pinhead dance number and you got to thinking real deep now, way in there with the hand up for the ventriloquist shtick, opening wide the implanted white chompers clackin' and going on at a rate, oh what a big mouth you have, all the better to take you in, move it around just a li'l bit, please, please be my little, and you be thinking of the family pack shipping this hit outta here, flat wallet back pocket, wondering where exactly that was on the cliff-hang of things, riding on the thermals, hawk-like voracious, to set your claws, talon grip of the straightaway road...a fine late afternoon, just ripe for a glass of red wine and a complimentary hors d'oeuvres of paté on perfectly baked fresh bread, overlooking the lake and its water-borne traffic of yachts, sailboats, pleasure crafts, commanding a smart salute from the quarterdeck and from the foredeck in an array of pert bikinis, muff shaves, appropriate waxes, the man in the top hat dizzies the quayside patrons with a zoo of rabbits pulled from, pigeons from, and a startle of doves from, while below-deck hob knobbing continues, where the Transportation Minister is transported, unseen but suspected by the wide-eyed applause of dockside patrons, meanwhile back at the ranch the lone hero, armed with brushes and oil colour, gets lost in the crux exchange, where the lone gesture misses the mark when the bull's-eye gets moved, adjusted, "a New Configuration for a New Time," where the only possible is a reinvention of old adages, wives' tales, common sense, street smarts...

For Her mandatory Rear Double Bicep with Open Hands She poses without props or high heels before a gold curtain in a red two-piece suit that sets off Her tanned toned athletic body with left leg extended and arms raised to display the ripple of biceps trapezius and deltoid muscles while showcasing Her femininity muscle tone and the beauty flow of Her physique for the judges to score Her overall aesthetics and look found in figure competitions but with a little more muscularity

Divided we stand, united we fall

Lone-wolfing night streets unplugged from the intractable quotidian with your bow and arrow the telltale whizz as it strikes in the eye to the shock and horror of breaking news quickly broken for an honour roll served on a clean white platter as a takeout from the baked-goods store right next to the broadcast station, having taken lessons in cake decorating to suit the neighbours, the emulation, the copycatting, grovelling face-pressings for the big lick, when in all that time it was a simple turning your back, to face north, where lights appear along the spoor path to clearings ringed coniferous in the deep arboreal, where cleansing rites bring about the expulsion of virus breath, numbing of pox cocks, ululations to release death rattles of trophy-hunted fur bearers, consumption fire of wooden churches, sparks uprising in the night, fireflies of pain to burn, to die black-embered for ash spread in a vast osmosis of healing your wound that blackens your present ship to shore, and you'd go over to the Sip 'n Bite for the 99¢ Breakfast! and you think you'd get the penny back, no way, every time you gotta ask, where's my penny, looking like an asshole for asking, pissin' me right off all the time, having to deal with this petty dragging, having to think about it, deal with it, you got things to do, it's not easy street, friend…

The beloved buyer

You need frites, golden frites, side-plated with a Porterhouse medium rare, sauced with an exquisite Béarnaise. After you've grilled, while the meat settles, you sprint to the local franchise to place your order (you can taste the succulence, imagine the pool of *jus*, the drip of sauce), then stand aside to wait. Another customer places his order for a "coupla Gangbangs."

The cashier, a young girl, looks to the kitchen for help, where a cook nods, replies, "Chicken between two beef patties." She does the addition. He pays.

Your order up, you hotfoot home to the medium rare slathered with a warming Béarnaise along with frites now not quite so special, so juicy, so piquant, so tasty. How that guy smiled close-up before he laughed. To actually think this out. To be a thing, an openly laughed-at thing in front of that cashier—or was that the point? Barb-hooked by the world as it is, do you put up with it, shut up with it…? Your innocence shocking even to yourself, what yet you do not know, cannot imagine until now stuck, playing, earworming this rapacious bone of contention.

All good men

You thought, believed even, they were all good chaps from proper schools cushioned with blue chips, agreeable bank accounts: dedicated to an overarching view, a chain of being, of service and duty considerations, sympathetic understandings, inclusionary parties: the veil was lifted, an up-skirt photograph shocking and rude, clusters in backrooms, hands shaken, smiles and smirks exchanged, tacit backstabs, money rapes, plunders, pork barrelling, mutual backslaps, knife thrusts, "You too, Brute-Boy"...

Trudging in a blizzard along Bloor Street, walking faster than the gridlock of automobiles, weighted with boots, long johns, overcoat, scarf, toque, and a freezing wet face, shoulders hunched up to your ears. Reaching Bedford Road, slow-stepping into the silence of the Annex: lace patterns of snow-laden branches, unwalked paths through Taddle Creek Park, up Admiral Road. Yellow light of street lamps through falling snow, softened edges, lumps of benches, blurred road and sidewalk. Long serene silence. To stand there. To know your country is winter, soft, plump, quiet. To stand alone in this, your white world. You have survived, you have made your way, you have words for this, you have fashioned a life outside the snow fence of their governance, you have stepped your first step into the snow blank field, made your mark. You are reverent in your belittlement to wind and snow, to your ancestors in the face of this wilderness, huddled in their sod houses around the candlelight in the midst of the howling expanse of blinding white...

"Ya, up dere near da Jaworski, by da vindbreak dat focking horse; I'm going shoot it."

You are reclaimed, refreshed, the vapour of your breath upward upward, assailing upward garlic-snapping Bohunk booze-swilling Mick raiding the garden party, stomping across the lawn, upsetting the tea-cakes...

Old boys in private-school drag, their faces pancaked, lipsticked, permed wigs, eyeliner, mascara, full-throated dresses to disguise Adam's apples, lip-synching in the Christmas Masquerade from a rack of Edisonian wax cylinders: "We will, we will screw you," sadistic experts, summa cum laude of thievery, blackmail, pickpocketing, and the quick kick to your genitals for the excitement of a diversion, a look the other way. I che plus I che equals touché...

That would sweep away fundamental
hand-brought things

Vainglorious upraising of your arm brandishing sword, rifle, bayonet, and flag: an island in no-man's land where the streets of gold, the yellow brick road, turned to river stones with blood-run rivulets reflecting bullet-pocked walls, shells of buildings: pathetic wallpaper, scorched paint, shattered roof beams, odd shoes, a doll's head and body bloat in the gutters. Cracked voices from the PA system intoning a floss of fantasy in the lurid colours of a down-at-the-heels circus, flea ring, merry-go-round, organ-grinding fervours of God-bended kneejerks, saliva sly, greasy and oily posing for turns, struts, white-gloved hand waves downstage from the cardboard and painted sets of sunrises and wheat fields to enforce a servitude of Dark Age squalor over the mud-hut floors, gut-strung beds, pot-battered kitchens where the stick-finger twig fire dies below this week's grass soup and potato-peel pie, clubbed and scrapped over from the dining rooms of bins behind the Château Laurier. In fields where they lay in wait for a blood rage of beatings, for the audacity to show up, rag-dressed, bootless, and haunted, propped up on the crutches of baptisms, confirmations, holy chrisms, sacred grey ashes, wine and bread of the divine and noble flag waving and swishing gold raiment of God's most holy bestowing from pulpits, balconies, stone steps, plazas with pomp and pump...

This wasn't some time lapse unfolding of a flower frill of its petals can-can dancing into fragrance and colour to show, to offer itself, to become a poem, to be a metaphor, a burgeoning but an infold shrinking into itself, sucking away from sunlight, drying its delicacy, its softness become hard, brittle, moisture evaporated into sharp edges a small tight fist, without heart surge in the lift of spring.

"What?" said the criss-crossed christ. "You think I'm hanging around for your adorations, genuflections, some abstract mimicry of my suffering with yours? Get off it! Nails? They used rusted ones. Hurt? Holy shit, you could take it to the bank. And what do you know, that entire atomic mushroom, that black cloud ascending off the face of the earth, not to mention that miasma of fumes, to hit the vault of heaven. Dad had to hand out gas masks. And I'm going through this expiation for the stunning quality of your blighted inability to get along. When all the joy of what you could have obliterated by commands, rules, strictures in my name; all that snaking of a Hollywood morality play, continuous affirmation, reinforcement in the confines of the gated community you'd so studiously built around the fear of "who's the bottom." Feeling so good you could lay (if you'll pardon that verb) foundations for the edifice of payback, mortgages, usury on labour's bent back tied, chained, handcuffed to the kids; a Gordian knot you made while we gave you a bit of joy, to take you out of time; it feels good, that brain blast of dopamine, causation of desire, to be the need you want and then restrict its access to a routine of the same old same old, despite the evidence of the priests (the very arbiters) in the whorehouse, predatory inoculations of an altar boy's bum, and then you tell me, incarnate member of the trinity, with the prohibition and constructed morality tale of:

You know what you're gonna get where you're goin'... Yeah... Some T-R-E!!
T-R-E...?
Yeah, traumatic rectal enlargement!

Which wasn't the thing at all, because you hadn't added the water to come clean. Your reinforced perspective to paint it as pain in the ass, while ignoring the historical memory of fact that this hasn't been going on for thousands of years because it hurts. No, this wasn't it at all, what it is is a put-paid-to of your construction, seemingly inconvertible hetero (thrusts in stiff, flops out limp) scaffolding to get paid in bondage by building on the nakedness of birth, on the need for shelter, necessity of food, despite my sermon on the freedom of birds and the multiplication of buns and fish and yes, that is metaphoric parable. Your abject nudity at the moment of your first breath and scream gripped in the tightwad of a banker's fist, when the first money lender stepped on the bent backs to claw, kick, and scramble to the top of the pile, the tip of the architectural model, now social model of the pyramid. Fuck you and your prayers."

(Whaaat?)

One whole swamp of an excretory dump welling up on the vision of those who act on impulse, uncontrolled, a never knowing of a turn to the left or right, tearing down a structure of song, impetuous dance, stomping to rhythms borne up from ditches, gullies, riverbeds, and roiling springs, from the far edge of town before the naming of soul, before the structures of dead forms, before the bumblings of speech to vast, uncharted seas and territories, unfenced deserts and grasslands, from the dark forest, from the glaciered peaks, from the soft fold of valleys, down to the bottomland, from the heights of the highland, you flew.

A yellow-peaked red-starred head-
band holds in place a massive wig
of black curls falling over Her bare
shoulders with a crimson bustier eagle-winged across Her bust
with a yellow belt transitioning to
dark blue and white star-spangled
skin-tight briefs over nude panty-
hose leading down to high white-
striped red boots posed before a
fireplace in a front room a pearl
earring peeking out from Her left
ear as white as Her teeth set off
by the red-lipsticked smile Her
braceleted arms akimbo slightly
turned to the camera costumed as
Wonder Woman and ready to go

How many pictures, films, lectures were attended before the societal model in which we live had been superimposed on us by the architectural model of the pyramid? Not an imaginary point, the top place to succeed to, but an actual climb to a viewpoint, the tip, standing on the shoulders of lower blacks browns reds and yellows, even the heads of those, in a false below, where their endurance, steadfastness, ability to shoulder pain was bent to the service of those who'd stepped, clawed, kicked, and climbed with the support of all those now nominated as "them" or "others," being only a slight lingual shift from the old, more direct phrase "lower orders," with shoe treads marking their faces. All fine and dandy if you're standing, arms waving free at or near the top, with a complete arrogant sensibility to the trajectory, the arc of those lives lived in their now-characterized, abject positions, being merely an observation from above, including the memorial erasure of where the tip-tops arose from themselves in a mostly convenient loss of short-term memory, cushioned as they are by the ability to purchase the most precious commodity of all: distance from their roots (i.e., their shitting, pissing, and rutting), as if these functions were of an elevated nature above their very natural connection to their now most holy adored and coveted bodies ("O, vile bodies!"), which we in our condition confer upon them in Möbius strips of our own seemingly unending twist in the recognition of our imposed and accepted condition, while knee-bending to this pretense to false royalty, an already questioned position available only by chance, throw of the dice, planned parenthood, or in other endeavours as described by the phrase "cream rises to the top," while entirely neglecting that cream, fat heavy, rises from mere milk squeezed either manually or by induced vacuums of mechanized milkers from an increasingly abstract udder, fed by the ruminations of grass, which in this written form arises, finds expression through the necessary act of breathing itself while toking another meaning of the descriptor "grass."

But wait! Floods, both Biblical and historical, rising waters, or in this case, the milk of human kindness, washing at the ankles of the lower orders, rising ankle, calf, thigh, submergence of the points of interest, filling the navel, only if it's an innie, for outies a disappearance of that tiny blimp, and a quavering of the support system, becoming shaky in its foundations, nipples, aureoles, teats lost to view in the rising white, collarbones, shoulders, Adam's apples, necks...

"Who's staying around for this, get swimming!" Australian crawls, sidestrokes, breaststrokes, dog paddles, and butterfly... "We're outta here!" as the bottom layer **("Of all things, the audacity, I've never seen such cheek in all my born days!")** swims free, every man, woman, child for themselves, in a complete abdication of their station as the first layer, read bottom or tranche, disintegrates, not merely in structure but definitely in laws, morals, norms: finances begin falling into the milk without any kindness at all, levelling the entire mass to a horizontal head-bobbing similarity, egalitarianism, evening out the false trope of the level playing field, which it now was until the inevitable separations began once more between the crawlers and the paddlers, now forming particular swim clubs and setting in yet once again an "us and them" swim meet based on litheness, kickboxing skills, and this season's colour of bathing suit **("Don't you dare peek at those nudies!")**, ignoring for the time being the condition of exhaustion soon overcoming one by one, club by club, no matter the chosen style, to treading in the milk of human kindness but not for long, as is, of course, our condition...

The bee in the bonnet: buzzing, tormenting, in danger of inflicting a sting, so you want to capture it in a bottle of chloroform, and when dead and no longer dangerous, pierce it with a pin stuck into a little glass-sided box for inspection and show it off along with the wall-mounted antlers. (**"See, I told you what would happen."**)

Men with their arms around the shoulders of thousands and thousands, breathing a singular darkness into the vault of a deaf heaven, goose-stepping into the bottom footnote that will not record their names, marching abreast, staccato of their boots in unison, flags wind-whipped and snapping, voices raised in song and salute, quick-stepping to the precipice of history, a roll of dice for the return to the women-who-wait for their knuckles and knee bones.

Her body arched with head turned to look over Her shoulder She poses standing on Her left leg Her right leg extension en pointe for Side Triceps with Extended Leg right arm back down hand hidden behind the right thigh Her arc stretches Her red V-bottomed bikini over Her vaginal bump shows upper leg hip flat stomach outline of rib cage Her red cupped breasts push out to expose one side of Her breast whiter than Her overall tan turned perfectly for the judges of the Women's Physique where none of Her family attends

Familiar plans

And then the plan, the exercise, the two to tango where one + one = any number, engine and driver of the dynamic, the action, known places, saying yes to the shuffle between one and one by shotgun, saved face, maid and master and some little bastard, you me and baby make three, liquor consumed to drench the anger became the spirit to the flame, rack and thumbscrews to dole out pain and measure pressure brought, to assuage, to pay what could not be but paid already in the marrow ate and eat a most civilized devouring where one wants out. About the hand that feeds you in translation mouthing the bite feeding on you with the full clench of the original friction that offered up birth as problem solver: "I'ma gonna givya twelve inches of the bestest in town—i.e., four inches thrice and everything nice…"

Overriding dialogue of tyrant and tantrum a barely disguised matter-of-factness, a status quo, a two-way street, a lane of sufferability, a taking-in, a soaking of an interior sponge when at the time of dish and serve its contents squeezed out to be served back to its rightful owner with neither a need nor a want but a take-back to where such matter belongs. These waylaid plans, familial plans, hard won in the battle planned without lines, warfare, and friction, no clear sight, no open field, jungle of half truth, insinuations, catechisms of superstition with "thou shall nots," these family plans planned and executed of the entire deed undone ash to ash and where to put them thrown in the face of one + one mingling, commingling, a get-together, a chatter of voices, a clatter of cutlery with everybody there on the lawn in the chairs with dinner together, laughter and prattle and something else underlying a bass note solid for not acknowledged, unspoken about, the random plan offspring and offshoot, a litter of chances, what were the chances, this sorrow, this rip in the mask, this question unasked, unexpected, something nasty bubbles from a lake bed, a snatch at the corner of an eye, a fish hook in the finger, hands on the wheel, foot stomping on the gas, Her muscle car driven into an oncoming Freightliner, ear-splitting grind of metal, explosion of headlights on metal, terror-widened eyeballs, damages and lawsuits, unscathed walk-away, a rehearsal of things yet to come and you bend this way and that, never look back in this pretend, this end, this hide with seek, this kick of the can planned, siblings, rivalry, under the moon madass and badness brought on by the abuse from a number of men and the question that hangs there, stills air: "What do we do to the women...?"

The beloved buyer

Can I help you?

Yeah, I just—

I'm with a customer right now; I'll be back in five…

Okay…

(going on 10) (12)

Hi, sorry about that… What can I do?

I've misplaced my charger for this phone, can I get another one?

Let's see… Oh, we don't have that phone, only the new ones.

I bought it a year ago.

Yeah, we can't keep all that in stock.

But you sold it to me; there were ads on TV.

We have new ones.

But they were a hundred dollars each. I got two of them with no charger…

Yeah, sorry 'bout that… You could try—

I've done that, this is the sixth place I've tried. This company sold it to me…

Yeah…

Do you have any Vaseline?

Excuse me?

T-R-E!!!

ask my ass / ass backwards / ass crack of dawn / ass in a sling / ass is grass / ass man / ass on the line / ass over teakettle / ass whipping / ass wipe / bad ass / bare ass / bet your ass / big ass / bite my ass / bring ass to get ass / bust or break ass / candy ass / can't find his ass / chew ass / cover your ass / crawl up your ass / cut ass / drag ass / from ass to appetite / get in someone's ass / get it in or up the ass / get one's ass in an uproar / get one's ass up / hang it in your ass / hang somebody's ass / have one's finger head nose up somebody's ass / hold ass / how's your ass / in somebody's ass / jump up my ass / kick ass / kiss my ass / lose ass / munch my ass / not on your ass / on somebody's ass / out the ass / pain in the ass / piece of ass / pull something out of one's ass / shake ass / shut your ass / stick it up your ass / suck my ass / take it in the ass / talk like a man with a paper ass / tear somebody a new ass / the sun sets in or out of somebody's ass / up somebody's ass / up the ass / your ass / your ass is in the wind / your ass is mud / your ass sucks buttermilk

Daddie wa daddie on the bounding main
and the binding maim

After the good doctor smeared carefully, he gingerly eased himself and waved goodbye thirty minutes later...set upon the road, wind at your back, journey, voyage, *viaje*, in the distance another voyageur, a figure there bivouacked in the arboreal, a sailor from the seas, match strike breaks the night, you draw to the flame, Onan presents for a clearing... Now voyager, now sailor, and he giveth, bends unto the altar to offer and burn both ends...

In spite of his bottom...turning...turning...coming up, every man saw the first clear sight they had of him: he was one, under cover of the moonless night. No great spread, his tired rig to the breaking point, the warm pink standing to the bone; one of the crew explaining, questioning, anticipating.

What lay behind? His rows of ports open to a slight movement that he was about to lay and wait for them. He got close enough to squat. He had lost a topman in the last blow. He had responded, but outgunned, they could take him to keep him broadside and maul him terribly and rake him right along the length of him. He could make almost no reply. It could be done: it had been done. With long ones between them able to open his lower ports, running high, to engage, to get one off, but for how long? See what you can make and you do with wind and wave, rope-burned fingers and callused palms, "Hold fast."

Long-legged shipman had finished spreading and his "Aye-aye, sir" came down black and pelting, so thick, long, uncut. While the men, spouting in the pale gleam, hulled up and fished him good, real good, he made a lewd gesture, one hand going with smiles all around.

"Take it off," flushing dark red, "take it right off." "Now, if you please," grunted, he fished his main, standing bare, hauled up and ready.

Now clear above the jagged edge when the swell raised, he wiped the streaming, swung round, snapped and gazed back at the distant holy when they were not looking. He so wanted but still fluid: more a potential than a situation. Any decision now began to take shape, moving at first slow and then faster and faster, never to be undone but made, made quickly in minutes. Yet there, close-hauled, the turning would hold him back right across his course: he might have to make another, the urge upon them. **("Did you say urge, the urge that crosses boundaries?")**

The feeling of those on his back: several officers and a couple of civilians. Not long ago, he had taken it: it had been the talk for some months. It made the decision less difficult... "More, please!"

Standing with a noncommittal look, smoothly changing and so close beside him, and with so little room, talking in a language by some eagerly, then leaning down to whisper in his ear... "Wanting you in the cockpit any moment now." You are about to...you want to.

Duck up, gather speed and come racing... At last there came the quick, the careful laying, the swirl eddying, briefly waving, a combined speed, fast and beautifully handled, rising and falling on the swell. A row of brown knowing faces grinned for a few moments of backing and filling up the stern, it flowed back and spread throughout, a full-throated howl of joy and delights with ecstasy in their depths vanished in a puff of smoke. What signal he had been about to make, of the severe control imposed upon his face... His tone invited lust.

"It is charming how sensible of the blessings," by way of private means paid off in a thoughtful leaving. He would have shown more pleasure looking at him. "Put it down to the anxieties of the night, the long strain, the apprehension in a fine flow, but whatever happens, he goes."

Drawing in a sharp breath no less, he was broad as well as tall. He let his breath out in a sigh... No great likelihood to cruise, this infernal making of a six-month run. Such a run when I was a boy: a prodigious boom vang that could really hold within the remembrance of things long past.

At first glance startling and unrecognizable She looks up into the camera wearing a widow-peaked pale blue hoodie with dark blue eye shadow bleeding down Her face over Her black lipstick Her eyes marbled Her face dark hard smeared and messed

"To tell you the truth, I don't remember his name who had such a trying time with a moist palm, but by naming would give a subtle hint of the position." The name would not come, so he reverted to the advertisements. "A great deal to be said with three or four within reach, a day's ride for a dozen. Ask some of the young ones to come, I should like it of all things."

Pole aches down, cold over: breathing up, across, up and up to that great sweep, open down on the lower reaches. A score far away and below, his motionless behind through the furze and the brown. Slow work; patchy scent blow, winding through, scattered along and far away. There knew dwindling of his stream in the hope of catching a glimpse, both tied. Had been led astray early: he could not resist the horn, the scent had faded and died... His finger, his pulse paused... Some reprieve, on the far side a figure. A strange air about him: his pale face, his dark eyes, his close-cropped skull, his slender bone-white rubbed with recognition. "I tell you what it is. It's those goddamned rutting dogs. Now get on with it."

Pursed his lips and pushed, leading round out of sight: they have found their fox. Sat naturally upon it, red round up eagerly into the furze, where heave and rustle showed the pack in familiar cluster motion...

*

Relax...relax...deeply relax, from the tip of your toes to the top of your head, feel your feet rest and your ankles relax, your legs relax, relax, your hips sink deeper into the couch, relax, your stomach and chest release their tension and your arms relax, your neck gives way and relaxes and your head sinks deeper, relaxed...relax now...relax...

Bill payments, return calls, invoice shortfalls, estimates of critical paths, amounts owing, due dates and deadlines, the number of keys on your ring, the doors they open securely closed, groceries garnered, dirty dishes, laundry folded, floors swept, beds made, their drag weight lifting, shoulder pain subsiding into the couch, resting, and a long seemingly blank wait for whatever to take their place under rise from the quotidian entrapment, follow through and avoidance now erupting upward, quick takes at the corner of the eye lost in the dailies, stronger now and a tangible required, a handhold to grip onto in the vacant swaying, toe tips on the cliff edge, the welling dark now and where you are, pit stomach fear revolts for the coming pinpoint lightening in the toss turning half-remembered animation colour of that dream weave, forgotten in the awakening, now bearing straight ahead all forward-ho unto the altar, all day deeds done and performed mutual well-oiled and roiling into unto out to in and out two palm slip oil slide sluice over blades, glutes, pecs, pits, under and around whipping extension bone play joy toss offering hole spread invitation, emboldening, embedded, wraparound, deepening warm press folding thrust in string connection multiples in a ring-around, in arboreal forests, sand plains, hedgerows, stone ruins, abandoned buildings, ill-lit parks, dark-ended doorways: where there, on edges over night places, enacting full-throated throttling of some straight sad daily, outright outlaw outré, *la seducción, los abrazos, los besos, los orgasmos, la leche,* milk of manly and the way opened...

*

She stood on a sliver of moon, hands steepled in the received gesture of prayer, her eyes, O look...her eyes not downcast but wide-eyed staring, no, in shock across the stone-laid courtyard over and through arboreal figures and bloom-filled bushes and bedraggled begonias... You looked, searched about you for the resting spot of her gaze, no not that really, but her stare, the blazed spear points hard upon some bull's eye, where you looked, decided to place yourself under her figure, look to where she looked...the alignment...and there to the right a marble basin with a bull nose return around the rim that looped upward on the far side... In the loop a bearded face with a wide O mouth where water once flowed... First stirrings begin their pinprick along rising warmth...perhaps a possibility furtive and sneaky...the basin dry and the backpack with your kit (cock ring, lube, and poppers)...the alignment and quick pics on the mobile for site sharing...immediate hits...a scroll to see who's closest...and there you are...

This goat-footed construction from remnants, slow accretion...two full tokes only after the site is prepared...a remembering of when... each revel and glimpse tied in...a self-exploratory in loosening broad reaches with a jibe or two in ripples, waves, whitecaps, all in one for this afternoon's tsunami...and for this moment, free from time's daily netting...

Rustle of bunch grass, banks of greenery just before the crest in a rising flood of encouragement for another tight return offering... The arboreal forest in thicket hid, pink and white, sun-pierced gloom... Giveth this thy daily and come unto me this gift of cupped palm to hold dark at bay brought white.

It took about a month, the safely alone month, clothes optional, kicked in the corner with another grip on...three days and it's time for an addition...another strategic grip...pain released incorporated... A couple more days, there's a yawn with an itch...slippery and deft and Pony Express, tying them together in the rhythm wreck of deep song... Another day...lubed hand succeeds, its grasp in slow movement of a beginning time, incremental, bit by bit, into the initial pleasure-roam...

A waiter, with his tray, leans against the bar to pick up his drinks order, replenishes your champagne, whispers, "I wanna tie you up," then whisks away with a wink and a smile.

You need the little death...want the little death...so inappropriately named, this appropriation of freedom...to divest all those diversions air-brushed and colour-saturated, curling their come-fuck-me fingers at you...for the grand replacement of intimate infancy coupled with an orgasm...showboated and drawn out of the top hat, plastic to platinum with wingbeats of buy-buy-'n'-purchase, that's why you're here.

The beloved buyer

"Look at those pillows on display!"

And with enough purchase appeal, you enter the boutique. You are greeted with chiclet smiles and appraising eyes, the purr before the pounce. You want one! Those agreeable colours in a Mid-Century Modern biomorphic form in muted orange, olive, cream. You clutch it to yourself, take it to the cash desk, things becoming warm, fuzzy, near erectional, beloved while you are clientelled: full name, complete address, email, Instawham and NikNok accounts, and what hand you use.

You got it home…a colour clash looking stupid all by itself on the expanse of couch, lost, bereft, a reflection of yourself. You're gonna haveta pay for the whole damn display to repair your ensemble, the vignette you imagined, an aspiration, a desire, an accomplishment where you palm-cuddle and wrap yourself while you seize, clutch, grip, before this attainment, this small comfort, flies, flits, flees, evaporates, for you to become as you now realize, end loser, forlorn as a box of Kleenex next to the laptop's effervescent screen, bio and morphic.

Meanwhile back at the bunkhouse
with the deckhand

Then stripped and shoved on low for an hour, a long hot, and went down for a night visit, no choice. A random something calling itself solid ranging back over and pulled a couple thick in my fingers top and bottom down in leather wrapped totally exhaustive of every known technique for another solid hour, the introduction ever stolen but flipped, trawled twice, three times, into untidy sprawl going back to the big red time and time again, a hell of a buzz with shock and excitement from beginning to end, from top to bottom, from inside out...a simple jumping blazed over the night look of sweatshirt and boxer briefs with something to show in the bathroom... Better be damn good, and then he joined you...one hell of a voyager, that one.

His eyes in the glow, what it's all about, glanced over again, "Want to see where to go?" Surprise on his face and told him and hurtled into light spilling the fierce behind with a start me off and a faint beginning glimmer as tight as slowed and swung, getting stronger, all that last night taken down, slowed, swivelled and swung, mashed and hummed a gasp to play with and whooped at each other high-five speeding until bleached and blank... No doubt about that, this is something else with their pants down and hanging out... "Did you figure this out?" Hoisted us through gathering sprawl, busy confirming a growth in strength to show you stuffed, reinforced by good schooling before the final, the only place to find a stash in his own place, a loop around and a liquid ribbon in the soft morning.

For a moment without a word and pushed the point under the top, an avalanche poured out, crumpled, loose and fluttering, two random fistfuls held up, dim, small, and beautifully dirty in the pale morning, big hands full, and we looked at each other and started swishing hands, the air thick with it, whooping and slapping, smacking around on the bathroom floor... We rested, panting, leaned into the sun seat to face a huge scale, a mass production the next red light, the bleaching thing a mass of stuff in the zone.

Took off into a big case, making things tricky down there, sniffed out four more last night, the backup crew right behind you, give me twenty down there, went up to see what would happen, they came to nail me and I took them like a dog...a twenty-year-old pulled indecent. "How the hell with a thing like this? It's his fault with what he's got to do." Never say no to the honey, a hell of a lot of honey, right down to who polishes the cherry...bad luck or no luck at all in the right place, a run on down up in the slot laid on top his over that stool... What do we do...we take it... He was holding it rock-steady and pointing it, to tiddly the wink.

A strong feeling this was going to the last, a stand up and move over sideways, his hand up under the weight, side by side, heart breaking, a bone face without a smile, a fat silence getting close, sneered out of his blank, fiddled and clicked, withholding the winning hand. A rising note of regret in the playing out... It hadn't started out this way, nothing immediate, it came later slowly. It was always a chance either way to close the gap or not...and then what? Pain clench of his beauty under the lamplight and the rise of desire there, with words dry-coughed at the back of your throat...

To be a Daddie with all that that entails, to listen, to advise, to hold you cuddled, to undress you, whispering in the crook of your neck, to begin in innocence and follow in the lay of what intimacy brought of each two, need and want, but bring... To whisper of many things, of ravages and we two kings... Oh, such a thing...such a thing!

It crowds in hotfooting until your feet run cold, a frozen transparent block of ice in hindsight dead in your tracks... What you did and didn't do and how you long for him...

Gotta be white boxer briefs, the kind that tighten up across your and extend down your: when you bend over, it stretches and you can see the dark spot, that place that's going to draw a lot of attention...two tokes into it and a popper huff, it's demanding attention, jelly...(Talkin' 'bout jelly)...on the right latexed hand and slip those underpanties down just like the good doctor did and put the ointment there with a little push and breathing a sigh for the beckoning and a reach around to smear the Pony Express...smear the Pony Express... Twenty bucks and it doesn't talk back...that slight preparatory resistance before the unfolding and the indescribable slide: he was so good lifting and begging the night signalled by how he took your undies down, slipping off your extended legs and dropping them on the floor or best, tearing them apart and throwing them over his shoulder to stick-shift from first to overdrive...long-gone memory tightgripped... Like him, you do do and do like him, with your free hand at the nippled power buttons...suction the pony to the floor and wet up the right hand for the so tense sticking beyond... Meld them together, knit the trinity of nipple dick and butt, bound as one... Climb aboard and go back there... Your ankles on his shoulders as he bends you back, bottom up, to finesse his way home, while he walks his hands up your body to lean in and French a tongue-lashing... Black body above white naked...pecs, abdomen hard and black above...all of it, black jokes, slurs, and put-downs, the spit word a wall to block his beauty... And you are close and he is here now now and now, here dropping on the floor, falling on the floor, glow-wormed an' easy...alone an' free at last...all too brief for what crowds in, erupts, breaks loose from under the surface of things to disturb the now of this present...

Looking directly at the camera wearing a black cardigan over a pale pink blouse that sets off Her flawless skin inherited from Her paternal grandmother She's on the verge of a smile not a hair out of place Her dark eyes softened She is so achingly beautiful

... Soliciting by the side of the road for gas money, put Her in a psych ward for three days, to be let out screaming obscenities, ending up in the street, throwing rocks through windows. You're on the stairwell landing put to the test, up or down, bedroom or basement in all of its forlorn and guilty pawing through Her drawers, cupboards, closets, nude photo albums, sweetgrass, makeup kits, wigs and costumes, divorce papers from Her marriage to a Hawaiian you never knew about. Her clothes rack split between everyday wear and night wear, outlandish, stereotypical coquette wear, pink-fringed leather, white go-go boots, a lattice-laced bustier and some come-fuck-me pumps that could attract the most wolfish fantasies of the most socially inept johns, losers, and the crippled sexuals with bad teeth She'd brought home for your silent frowning disapproval.

You descend to the basement and stand beside shelves of the ordered yearly financial records of Her massage business that went bust. Heaped in one corner: cardboard trays of shampoos, lotions, creams bought and paid for to begin a lucrative, home-based business of the most unattractive labelling, to guarantee their complete unsaleability but to allure Her inside this most successful fantasy of parting a person from their money. Scattered, dusty, and sullied by how pathetic this hope against their deep-end place in the beauty market, offering neither transformation nor redemption. The cheap, chemically scented, nauseous perfume not quite masking the smell. You turn to recognize, as you survey under the bare bulb, rope lengths snaked near the over-turned ladder below the well-secured galvanized pipe, between the pair of joists from which She hanged herself. A last confrontation to your family's determined denial to acknowledge the sprawl of Her sex life hurled back at you, complicit...

You slouch from the embrace of the restaurant, step 'n' gimp to the high Toronto tower, take the elevator and rise to the observation deck, limp onto the platform, raise your puny arms, shout to the east where it skirls around the Haligonian Citadel in Nova Scotia, flusters through Pocologan in New Brunswick, spindrifts athwart the outport harbours of Newfoundland, shifts to rappel along the ramparts of Quebec City, the Plains of Abraham, ruptures the silent hallways of Ottawa, scuds and weaves through Sault Ste. Marie up to the Laurentians, almost glaciates in Pangnirtung and Uluhaktok, freewheels across the Prairies of Manitoba and Saskatchewan to cuff heads of wheat, stampedes across Alberta to the foothills and scales over the Rockies to breeze through the Similkameen and Okanagan valleys, lifts over the Coast Range to fall twist spiral over the Fraser Delta to sift out over the Strait of Georgia to Victoria and finally cross Beacon Hill Park to spread wide over the Pacific...

"Please, oh please...forgive me..."

Acknowledgements

There are many people who deserve to be gratefully thanked for reading early iterations of the book you now hold in your hands.

Thank you to Ruth Zuchter for an early punctuation regimen. To Bev Daurio, who asked if she could read the manuscript and essentially stepped out of retirement to suggest, to guide, to help make this book so much better, I am deeply grateful. To Stuart Ross, who had seen an early version of this and didn't forget it when he created the imprint 1366 Books and to make it the kickoff. I am thankful to him—and to Guernica Editions—for making a space for "readable experimental prose."

To Juan Goytisolo, who taught me; I remain a humble pupil with so much yet to learn.

For all the Forester and O'Brian historic sea novels of the Napoleonic War from which I pirated phrases and grape-shotted sentences to inform my sailor, I am appreciative. As I am to Washington Irving for his story of Count Julian's daughter.   ·

My appreciation also to Derek Roberts, aka Dirty Swagger, for his permission to use the band name Dirty & the Derelicts, a band name sticker I found on Main Street, Vancouver, so perfect, so completely "right," I stuck it in a notebook hoping to use it and so I did, thank you!

To Aaron Tucker and Kirby, early readers and supporters in Toronto, and in Vancouver Meredith Quartermain, who early on understood how I used incomplete sentences, I thank them for their considered and insightful back-cover words with appreciations and gratitude.

Fidel Peña of Underline Studio deserves mil gracias for the blockbuster visuals on the front and back covers, muy bien...!

To my partner of forty-four years, Donald Irving, who gives me time to write while telling all within listening distance that "writers are weird..." and I am!

I thank and love you!!

Brian Dedora is author of over twenty titles of fiction, poetry, memoir, and various forms of visual work. Despite some publication in the mid-1970s, it was meeting bpNichol, who introduced him to visual, concrete, and experimental writing, that became Dedora's opening to write and explore his form of artistic practice with text, photography, and collage beginning in 1977. Dedora grew up in the Okanagan and has lived in Vancouver, Spain, and Toronto, which he currently makes his home.

Other Books by Brian Dedora

Box Set & Bloonz (Viktlösheten Press, Sweden, 2021–23)

Black-Tee & White-Tee (nOIR:Z, 2023)

Section 2—Special Breakdown Torque (Gap Riot Press, 2022)

Recycled and Phrase-O-Matic (nOIR:Z, 2021)

Plague Spot (nOIR:Z, 2020)

Diagrams for a Vaudeville of Poems (nOIR:Z, 2019)

Three Prongs a Trident (nOIR:Z, 2019)

Lorcation (Editorial Visor, 2015)

Lorcation (Book*hug, 2015)

Two at High Noon (Nomados, 2015)

Eye Where: A Book of Visuals (Teksteditions, 2014)

Lot 351 (Teksteditions, 2013)

A Few Sharp Sticks (The Mercury Press/Teksteditions, 2011)

A Slice of Voice at the Edge of Hearing (The Mercury Press, 2008)

With WK in the Workshop (Mercury Press, 1989)

In the Bushes Under the Bay Window (Pink Dog Press, 1989)

White Light (Aya/Mercury Press, 1987)

The Mouse (Curvd H&z, 1986)

A Table of Contents (Surrealist Poets' Gardening Assoc., 1985)

What a City Was (Underwhich Editions, 1983)

He Moved (Underwhich Editions, 1979)

The Dream, a Posteriori (Kontakte Press, 1976–77)

About 1366 Books

1366 Books is an imprint of Guernica Editions, launched in 2024 to bring to light two books of innovative but accessible fiction annually. Each title—whether a novel, stories, or microfictions—is a unique literary experience. Imprint editor Stuart Ross welcomes submissions of fiction manuscripts that challenge or attempt to redefine the boundaries of the genre. He is especially interested in seeing manuscripts of experimental fiction from members of diverse and marginalized communities. Write to Stuart at 1366books@gmail.com.

Exploding Fictions

Printed by Imprimerie Gauvin
Gatineau, Québec